Samuel French Acting Edition

This Bitter Earth

by Harrison David Rivers

‖SAMUEL FRENCH‖

Copyright © 2020 by Harrison David Rivers
All Rights Reserved

THIS BITTER EARTH is fully protected under the copyright laws of the United States of America, the British Commonwealth, including Canada, and all member countries of the Berne Convention for the Protection of Literary and Artistic Works, the Universal Copyright Convention, and/or the World Trade Organization conforming to the Agreement on Trade Related Aspects of Intellectual Property Rights. All rights, including professional and amateur stage productions, recitation, lecturing, public reading, motion picture, radio broadcasting, television and the rights of translation into foreign languages are strictly reserved.

ISBN 978-0-573-70899-2

www.concordtheatricals.com
www.concordtheatricals.co.uk

FOR PRODUCTION ENQUIRIES

UNITED STATES AND CANADA
info@concordtheatricals.com
1-866-979-0447

UNITED KINGDOM AND EUROPE
licensing@concordtheatricals.co.uk
020-7054-7200

Each title is subject to availability from Concord Theatricals Corp., depending upon country of performance. Please be aware that *THIS BITTER EARTH* may not be licensed by Concord Theatricals Corp. in your territory. Professional and amateur producers should contact the nearest Concord Theatricals Corp. office or licensing partner to verify availability.

CAUTION: Professional and amateur producers are hereby warned that *THIS BITTER EARTH* is subject to a licensing fee. The purchase, renting, lending or use of this book does not constitute a license to perform this title(s), which license must be obtained from Concord Theatricals Corp. prior to any performance. Performance of this title(s) without a license is a violation of federal law and may subject the producer and/or presenter or such performances to civil penalties. A licensing fee must be paid whether the title(s) is presented for charity or gain and whether or not admission is charged. Professional/Stock licensing fees are quoted upon application to Concord Theatricals Corp.

This work is published by Samuel French, an imprint of Concord Theatricals Corp.

No one shall make any changes in this title(s) for the purpose of production. No part of this book may be reproduced, stored in a retrieval system, or transmitted in any form, by any means, now known or yet to be invented, including mechanical, electronic, photocopying, recording, videotaping, or otherwise, without the prior written permission of the publisher. No one shall upload this title(s), or part of this title(s), to any social media websites.

For all enquiries regarding motion picture, television, and other media rights, please contact Concord Theatricals Corp.

MUSIC USE NOTE

Licensees are solely responsible for obtaining formal written permission from copyright owners to use copyrighted music in the performance of this play and are strongly cautioned to do so. If no such permission is obtained by the licensee, then the licensee must use only original music that the licensee owns and controls. Licensees are solely responsible and liable for all music clearances and shall indemnify the copyright owners of the play(s) and their licensing agent, Concord Theatricals Corp., against any costs, expenses, losses and liabilities arising from the use of music by licensees. Please contact the appropriate music licensing authority in your territory for the rights to any incidental music.

IMPORTANT BILLING AND CREDIT REQUIREMENTS

If you have obtained performance rights to this title, please refer to your licensing agreement for important billing and credit requirements.

This Bitter Earth was first produced by the New Conservatory Theatre Center in San Francisco, CA on September 22 to October 22, 2017. The performance was directed by Ed Decker.

JESSE HOWARD.................................... H. Adam Harris
NEIL FINLEY-DARDEN ....Michael Hanna

CHARACTERS

JESSE HOWARD – Late 20s–early 30s. Serious, passionate, Black. He wields his wit like a weapon. A playwright.

NEIL FINLEY-DARDEN – Late 20s–early 30s. Compassionate, privileged, white. He means well. An enthusiast.

SETTING

New York City, NY & St. Paul, MN

TIME

March 21, 2012 – December 15, 2015

AUTHOR'S NOTES

Style

Transitions between scenes should be fluid.
Fluid does not mean immediate.
Emotional truth is of greater value than logic.

1.

(Lights rise on **JESSE**. *He speaks out.)*

JESSE. Sometimes—and scientists may refute this, but fuck them—sometimes I can feel the Earth move. And not like tremors or earthquakes, tornados or hurricanes. This is not a matter of wind or tectonic plates, but rather a matter of chemistry. Body chemistry. *My* body chemistry. The inner workings of my inner ear. The rods and cones in my retina. The sensory receptors in my neck and ankles. Balance. Sometimes I can't get out of bed in the morning I'm so nauseous from the spinning.

On those mornings I require ginger ale. Sometimes that ginger ale also contains bourbon. It helps.

I find it strange that others can't feel it—the rotation. Strange and a bit lonely.

As you can probably imagine, my lack of balance has been difficult to navigate. Especially when I was a child. Walking, for example, was a chore. It involved such intense concentration that I developed migraines. I still get them.

(Beat.)

In moments of great pain—while in the throes of a migraine, for example—I think about something that the late great poet Essex Hemphill once said, "Take Care Of Yr Blessings," which he explained as our various gifts and talents. He said - some of us bake and some of us write. Some of us understand numbers or how to care for others. He said to be aware of what your particular things are and to nurture them and use them for good. And so in moments of great pain I think of my blessings and I count them.

One: I was given a mind and the ability to think
Two: I have the ability to put my thoughts on paper
Three—

> (*St. Paul, early December 2015. A street. Suddenly,* **NEIL**'s *arms are around* **JESSE**'s *waist. A cascade of words.*)

NEIL. Wait, wait, wait! How does it go again—?

JESSE. How do you not know this song? It's like essential—

NEIL. Essentially what? / And essential to whom—?

JESSE. What do you mean essentially what? / A proper education. A *basic* education—

NEIL. "Alabama, Alaska, Arizona, Arkansas…" / What comes after Arkansas—?

JESSE. I can't believe you went to private school—

NEIL. California! / "California—"

JESSE. Your parents paid like forty thousand dollars a year for twelve years and you don't know what comes after Arkansas?

NEIL. We didn't sing at Collegiate. We took fencing lessons.

JESSE. That's right!

> (**JESSE** *demonstrates his fencing skills.*)

Hi ya!

NEIL. More like—

> (**NEIL** *demonstrates his fencing skills.*)

En garde!

JESSE. Touché!

> (**JESSE** *slips on a patch of ice.* **NEIL** *catches him.*)

NEIL. Whoa there, Tiger!

> (**JESSE** *begins to laugh and then* **NEIL** *joins, though he's not completely sure why.*)

What are we laughing about?

JESSE. You just called me Tiger!

NEIL. What? NO! / I didn't—

JESSE. Yes, you did! Yes, you did! / I heard you—

NEIL. Why the fuck would I call you Tiger—?

(JESSE slips again. Both men react.)

JESSE.　　　　　　　　　　**NEIL.**

Shit! This fucking　　　　WHOA! Watch it—!
sidewalk!

NEIL. *(Continued.)* The last thing we need is a broken ankle—

JESSE. Or a broken knee—

NEIL. Or a broken arm—

JESSE. Yeah, or a broken butt!

(They find the prospect of a broken butt hilarious.)

NEIL. We definitely do not need a broken butt. I like yr butt the way it is. It's a nice butt.

JESSE. "Iowa, Kansas, Kentucky, Louisiana, Maine..."

(NEIL joins.)

JESSE/NEIL. "Maryland, Massachusetts, Michigan—"

(The sound of breaking glass. And then—NEIL is gone. St. Paul, mid-December 2015.)

JESSE. We had just left the bar. It was late. And cold. We could see our breath in the air. I remember we could barely stand we were so drunk. Fucking 3-4-1's. Neil had his arm around my waist for support and I was sort of leaning into him like you do when yr wasted and everything is loose and heavy. And I remember I slipped on a patch of ice. Twice, I think. I lost my already questionable balance twice and he caught me. He caught me. And he called me Tiger, which...well, he'd never called me that before. I remember I cracked the fuck up and then *he* cracked the fuck up and...

(Beat.)

We were both laughing when it happened. His left hand was here. His right hand was—

(The sound of breaking glass.)

2.

(West Village, March 2012. A diner.)

NEIL. Why do you have to say it like that—?

JESSE. What? Like what? / Like—?

NEIL. "Activist." Like you just put something disgusting in yr mouth—

JESSE. I didn't say it like that.

(NEIL gives JESSE a look.)

What? I didn't.

(Another look.)

What!

NEIL. I just think that sometimes it's hard to hear ourselves. You know, with all the *noise* between our ears or whatever.

JESSE. And I sound like I just put something disgusting in my mouth?

NEIL. Only when you said activist.

JESSE. You mean "activist."

NEIL. Be nice.

JESSE. I'm the nicest person I know.

(A shared smile.)

NEIL. All I'm saying, *jerk*, is that the way you said activist seemed to me to reveal a very clear opinion about activists. And I wouldn't even call myself an activist—

JESSE. Oh, come on—

NEIL. I went to one protest! / One!

JESSE. You were hanging off a statue! Waving a bullhorn!

NEIL. My first time!

JESSE. Whatever you say.

NEIL. I say... I find it hard to believe that yr not bothered by what you see when you look around. When you watch the news or read the paper. When you leave yr apartment.

JESSE. It's not that I don't understand the importance of protest or whatever, the importance of speaking up and speaking out. I know my history. I've seen *Eyes on the Prize*—

NEIL. But?

> *(Beat.)*

JESSE. I plead the fifth.

> *(**NEIL** smiles.)*

NEIL. You would.

JESSE. I just did.

NEIL. Yeah, well... I think you should reconsider yr stance.

JESSE. On?

NEIL. Activism.

JESSE. Don't you mean, "activists?"

> *(A shared smile.)*

NEIL. I told you, that was a...that's not what I do. I work in investments. Or... I did until recently.

JESSE. It didn't stick?

NEIL. I hated wearing ties. Plus, I only got the gig because of my father. And I only took it because of my mother so...

JESSE. So?

NEIL. So I'm happier now hanging from the occasional statue.

> *(Slight beat.)*

But what about you? You were there, too. Rallying, too. Wearing a hoodie.

JESSE. It was my roommate's.

NEIL. Oh, a detail. You have a roommate.

JESSE. Boy, this is New York City. Having a roommate is an economic necessity.

NEIL. Is she nice?

JESSE. *He* can be. We're in the same class at Columbia.

NEIL. Fancy.

JESSE. Hardly. I'm on scholarship.

NEIL. So yr smart?

JESSE. No, I'm just Black.

> *(Slight beat.)*

Sorry, that was… I haven't really spoken to anyone but my academic advisor about anything other than dramatic structure in like six months so my social skills… I'm afraid they're a little rusty.

> *(**NEIL** smiles and leans in.)*

NEIL. Trust me. Yr doing just fine.

3.

(St. Paul, August 2014. An apartment. **JESSE** *puts on a song in the style of Nina Simone's* **["BLACK IS THE COLOR OF MY TRUE LOVE'S HAIR"]***. *After a while,* **NEIL** *enters with a duffel.)*

NEIL. Seriously? This song?

JESSE. It's a beautiful song.

NEIL. Unquestionably. It is an unquestionably beautiful song, but it's also a dirge.

JESSE. It's a beautiful dirge.

> *(Beat.)*

NEIL. Jesse.

> *(**NEIL** turns off the music.)*

Come on, we talked about this.

JESSE. *You* talked.

NEIL. No, *we*, Jesse. *We* talked. *We* dialogued. *We* discussed. You said it was OK—

JESSE. I've changed my mind—

NEIL. Yeah, well, it's a bit late for that. The van will be here in five minutes and I intend to be on it.

---

* A license to produce THIS BITTER EARTH does not include a performance license for "BLACK IS THE COLOR OF MY TRUE LOVE'S HAIR". The publisher and author suggest that the licensee contact ASCAP or BMI to ascertain the music publisher and contact such music publisher to license or acquire permission for performance of the song. If a license or permission is unattainable for "BLACK IS THE COLOR OF MY TRUE LOVE'S HAIR", the licensee may not use the song in THIS BITTER EARTH but should create an original composition in a similar style or use a similar song in the public domain. For further information, please see Music Use Note on page 3.

(**JESSE** *turns the music back on.*)

Seriously? Yr being a child.

(**NEIL** *turns the music back off.*)

It's only a week—

JESSE. Oh, well when you put it like that. *Only* a week. / And don't call me a child—

NEIL. I'll be back before you know it—

JESSE. Cliché! / Cliché—!

NEIL. And you'll be in rehearsals anyway—

JESSE. Oh, so that makes it okay? That makes yr leaving okay? The fact that / I'll be in rehearsal—?

NEIL. That's not what I... Yr twisting my words.

JESSE. This is a fight, Neil. We are fighting. Of course, I'm twisting yr words.

NEIL. I don't want to do this. I'm practically out the door. I don't want to fight right before I have to go—

JESSE. *Have* to go—?

NEIL. Yes, *have* to. Plans were made. The "Freedom Ride" is on. Shit, I don't throw a hissy fit every time you tell me you can't do something because you need to write. I moved to Minnesota for fuck's sake. For yr career. For yr burgeoning writing-slash-teaching career. For *you*—

JESSE. That's completely different—

NEIL. How? How is it different? Support is support. And I've supported you. Yr thing. *This* is mine—

JESSE. Running off to Missouri with the "we are the world" tour / is yr thing?

NEIL. We're going to help.

JESSE. How? How are you / going to help?

NEIL. By being there. / By being available. By doing whatever needs doing.

JESSE. Bullshit / BULLSHIT!

NEIL. No, helping people isn't bullshit—!

JESSE. A busload of guilty white people—

NEIL. OK / *O-K*!

JESSE. White people trekking nine hours to Missouri to provide general assistance to hurting Black people? That, in my opinion, is some bullshit.

NEIL. That's not fair.

JESSE. Maybe not, but it's accurate.

(Slight beat.)

NEIL. Do you really not care? Is that it? You don't care about Michael Brown? / Or his mother? Or their community?

JESSE. This isn't about whether or not I care and you know it—

NEIL. Then what the fuck! The people in Ferguson are collectively having maybe the worst moment of their lives. The least we can do is stand with them.[*]

(Slight beat.)

I mean, come on, Jesse. "First they came for the Socialists and I did not speak out / because I was not a Socialist—"

JESSE. Yes, I'm familiar with the quote—

NEIL. Well then?

(Slight beat.)

JESSE. I just don't think / that—

NEIL. *(Pouncing.)* That what? / *That what*?

JESSE. Well, are you gonna let me finish or are you just / gonna keep interrupting me?

NEIL. Go on then! GO ON!

*(**JESSE** is silent.)*

You know, you accuse me of my white guilt, but what about yr apathy?

---

[*] The unrest in Ferguson, Missouri (Aug 9, 2014 – Aug 25, 2014) began after the fatal shooting of Michael Brown by police officer Darren Wilson.

(A long moment and then **JESSE** *turns the music back on.)*

Fuck, Jesse, look…

(A gesture, an attempt to make peace.)

There's room in the van if you want to come with me.

JESSE. I have rehearsals.

NEIL. Right. Right. Great. So now I'm an asshole for inviting you!

*(***NEIL*** picks up his bag and moves to the door.)*

I'm gonna wait outside. Do I at least get a goodbye?

*(***JESSE*** does not respond.)*

You know, yr not the center of the universe, Jesse. No one has that kind of gravitational pull. Not even you.

*(***NEIL*** exits. ***JESSE*** turns up the music, loud. And then he turns it off.)*

JESSE. Fuck.

5.

(St. Paul, late July 2014. A street. **JESSE** *and* **NEIL** *wave to* **JESSE***'s unseen parents.)*

NEIL. Nice to meet you!

JESSE. Love you! Travel safe!

NEIL. Oh my God.

JESSE. Holy shit.

NEIL. What was that? / What the fuck was that?

JESSE. Holy shit! Eamon and Sheryl Howard, ladies and gentlemen. Eamon and Sheryl Howard. Making things awkward—

NEIL. Awkward as fuck—

JESSE. Awkward as fuck since 1983.

NEIL. When did you say you came out again?

JESSE. High school. My sophomore year of high school.

NEIL. And they were *there* when you told them you were gay?

> *(Laughter.)*

JESSE. Shut up!

> *(Slight beat.)*

Fuck, I am so sorry. I am so so / so sorry.

NEIL. Please, they're the ones who showed up unannounced. In the middle of the night—

JESSE. Still—

NEIL. And whatever. It's fine. They were fine. Nice even.

JESSE. Yr sweet to say that.

NEIL. One question though: Is yr dad always so…?

JESSE. Baptist? Yes. Yes, he is—

NEIL. Oh my God, that prayer—

JESSE. "Father God, we ask that you bless this food to the nourishment of our bodies and that you bring a good Christian woman into Jesse's life."

NEIL. To fuck.

JESSE. Exactly. To fuck!

NEIL. Ah-men!

JESSE. A-men!

NEIL. Did you notice he found the Bible?

JESSE. Of course he found the Bible. Of course of all the books on all the shelves in that apartment he pulled down the New King James.

NEIL. And the whole sleeping fully clothed thing?

JESSE. Yeah, yr guess is as good as mine on that one.

NEIL. Do you think maybe he was afraid he'd get gay on himself?

JESSE. What?

NEIL. You know, sleeping in our bed. In our big gay bed—

JESSE. Our very big very gay bed—

NEIL. Could be traumatizing for a...

JESSE. For a what?

NEIL. A Baptist.

(They crack up.)

JESSE. I think my favorite moment was where he couldn't decide whether to hug you or to shake yr hand—

NEIL. We did sort of a hybrid thing, right? Like a half shake half hug—

JESSE. A SHUG—!

NEIL. YES, A SHUG! / Oh my God—!

JESSE. "When yr not sure how to engage yr son's boyfriend."

NEIL. "Do I hug? Do I shake?"

JESSE. "Try a little of both!"

(Beat.)

NEIL. Do you think they'll be okay getting on the highway?

JESSE. I'm sure they'll call if they get lost.

NEIL. Really?

(A moment and then—.)

JESSE. Please, God in Heaven. Guide my parents safely home.

NEIL. Ah-fucking-men.

JESSE. A-fucking-men.

6.

(NEIL speaks out.)

NEIL. A couple, maybe five years ago, Frank Rich interviewed Chris Rock for *New York Magazine*. In the interview Frank asked Chris if the election of Barack Obama meant progress and Rock said something like, "sure, for white people." And Frank was like, "for white people?" And Rock was like, "Black people have always been ready for a Black president. Like they never had any doubt that that was something they could do. Be president." Chris continued, "white people have progressed. They were crazy before. Now they're not as crazy."

And then he went on to talk about his daughters, who are smart and educated and beautiful and polite, AND YES, of a certain privilege, YES, but we can talk about that some other time because the point he makes, which I feel is a valid one, and one that is often lost in the discussion of black "v" white or whatever, is that there have been smart, educated, beautiful, polite Black children FOR HUNDREDS OF YEARS, right? And that THAT is not the NEW thing. NO. Rock said that the advantage now of now, NOW of NOW, is that his children are encountering the nicest white people that America has ever produced.

He said to Rich, "let's hope America keeps producing nicer white people." Nicer white people. That shit's both funny and true, which as far as I'm concerned is like the definition of good comedy.

(Beat.)

Sometimes when Jesse rolls over in the morning he'll say, "good morning, nicer white person." Or NWP for short. "Good morning, NWP."

He thinks it's fucking hilarious.

7.

(Brooklyn Heights, June 2012. A cab. **NEIL** *speaks to the unseen driver.)*

NEIL. Hi. Yeah, we're going to Harlem. One thirteenth and Frederick Douglass, please. Thanks!

*(***NEIL*** sighs.)*

What a night! You were great. My parents loved you, though I'm not surprised. My mom will be talking about those flowers for months. What were they called again?

JESSE. Ranunculi.

NEIL. Right, ranunculi. Gorgeous.

(Slight beat.)

I'm pretty sure yr the first boyfriend I've brought home who BROUGHT something with him. People used to have manners. Nobody has manners anymore. "Men are beasts."

*(***JESSE*** doesn't respond.)*

Hey, are you okay? Yr quiet.

JESSE. Yeah, I'm just tired.

NEIL. You can lean on me if you want.

*(***JESSE*** does. They ride.)*

You impressed my father. Yr the first boyfriend I've brought to the house whose face hasn't glazed over at the mention of Billy Collins or Joan Didion.

JESSE. Yeah, well he has great taste. And a great collection.

NEIL. He'll love you even more for saying that.

(Beat.)

JESSE. I Googled him.

NEIL. You…sorry, what?

JESSE. I Googled yr father. Before dinner.

NEIL. Um…why?

JESSE. Because you'd said like nothing about him. About either of them. And I didn't want to walk into the evening unprepared so I looked them up.

(**NEIL** *gives* **JESSE** *a look.*)

Don't look so shocked. I Googled you, too. Before we started dating.

NEIL. Yr not serious?

JESSE. Didn't you Google me?

NEIL. Why would I / do that—?

JESSE. Because knowledge is power and gay men are fucking crazy!

NEIL. Yeah, well I believe in giving people a chance.

JESSE. Oh yeah, me too. *After* I've cyber-vetted them.

(*A shared smile.*)

Apparently, you climbed some mountain? In California?

NEIL. I took a year off after high school and hiked from Mexico to Canada. Loads of people do it.

JESSE. Sure, but loads of people aren't profiled in *The New York Times*.

(*Slight beat.*)

Can I ask: Just how big is yr trust fund?

NEIL. (*Re: his dick.*) You've seen my trust fund—

JESSE. I'm serious, Neil.

(*A moment.*)

NEIL. Wait, is this why you were quiet during dessert? Because of my…?

(*Slight beat.*)

Look, Jesse. My family…we're just regular people—

JESSE. Regular people?

NEIL. Yes, regular people. My grandfather owned a construction company in the fifties. He made a little money—

JESSE. A little money! Neil, we just had a five-course meal. The wine served with dinner cost three hundred dollars a bottle—

NEIL. It was a special occasion—

JESSE. There were thirty more in the wine rack in the kitchen. I counted.

NEIL. Please don't make a big deal out of this.

JESSE. Seriously? That's yr response? Please don't make a big deal out of this?

NEIL. Yes, please don't. Because it really isn't.

(Slight beat.)

Are we seriously fighting about this—?

JESSE. No, this isn't a—

*(**JESSE** recalibrates.)*

I'm just...

(Slight beat.)

Why didn't you tell me?

NEIL. Tell you what?

JESSE. That you come from that. From a Brooklyn Heights brownstone and summers in Provence!

NEIL. It never came up.

JESSE. Because you didn't bring it up.

(Beat.)

NEIL. I wasn't hiding it from you.

*(**JESSE** gives **NEIL** a look.)*

I wasn't. I just...liked how things were going.

JESSE. Meaning me in the dark?

NEIL. No.

JESSE. Dating a complete stranger?

NEIL. Jesse, no, that's not—

JESSE. Not what?

NEIL. I just didn't want it to be a thing. Money has a way of becoming a thing and I didn't want it to be a thing.

JESSE. So you thought that if I found out you had money I would what? Try to steal it?

NEIL. No.

JESSE. Marry you and take half?

NEIL. Okay, now yr just being ridiculous / and mean—

JESSE. I don't want yr money, Neil—

NEIL. Yeah, well neither do I!

(They breathe.)

I thought we were having a good night.

(Beat.)

JESSE. You didn't tell them I was Black.

NEIL. I didn't...what? / That's not—

JESSE. Yr parents didn't know I was Black until they opened the door—

NEIL. What are you talking about? Of course they did. Of course they knew.

*(**JESSE** doesn't respond.)*

I told them. I know I told them. Or showed them a picture or...

(Slight beat.)

Okay, so maybe I... But I mean, it's not like they care.

*(**JESSE** gives **NEIL** a look.)*

What? They don't. They're not like that. They have a lot of Black friends.

JESSE. Jesus Christ, Neil, really? / They have a lot of Black friends?

NEIL. Sorry, no, that's not... That's not what I meant to say—

JESSE. You know what? Never mind. Forget I said anything about anything. Let's just go home, brush our teeth, turn out the lights and go to bed, okay? Great!

(They ride in silence.)

NEIL. Jesse—

JESSE. Nope. No talking.

NEIL. Jesse, please—

JESSE. What part of "no talking" do you not / understand?

NEIL. You can't just drop a bomb like this and then not let me respond.

(Beat.)

Jesse—

JESSE. Fine. Sixty seconds. Go.

*(**NEIL** takes a breath.)*

NEIL. My parents adored you. They did. When you left to go to the bathroom they practically fell all over themselves telling me how wonderful they thought you were. How wonderful they think you *are*. And they don't do that. They're honest people. Supportive, but honest. Brutally so. If they didn't like you, white, black, polka-dotted, they'd have told me. All that other stuff…the trust fund, Provence…it's bullshit, okay? Okay?

JESSE. Fine, it's bullshit.

(Beat.)

NEIL. You know what isn't?

JESSE. Isn't what?

NEIL. Bullshit.

(Slight beat.)

JESSE. *(Skeptical.)* What?

*(**NEIL** leans over and whispers in **JESSE**'s ear. It's probably something dirty. **JESSE** softens. They kiss.)*

8.

(Tribeca, April 2012. They move to the bed. Clothes are removed. Between kisses—.)

JESSE. Can I ask you a question?

NEIL. Right now?

JESSE. I swear it's relevant.

NEIL. Well, if it's relevant then by all means…fire away.

JESSE. Am I yr first?

NEIL. My what?

JESSE. Yr first?

NEIL. What, exactly? My first what, exactly—?

JESSE. Black dick, Neil. Black dick. Am I yr first / Black dick—?

NEIL. Oh. Sorry. Yeah. Yeah, I guess so.

JESSE. You guess or you know?

NEIL. Yes, yrs is my first. I hope that's okay.

JESSE. It's fine, obviously. Obviously, it's fine.

NEIL. Am I yrs?

JESSE. My first…?

NEIL. White dick?

(Slight beat.)

Sorry, that didn't sound nearly as sexy coming out of my mouth as it did coming out of yrs. Well?

JESSE. Not even close.

(The men re-engage.)

NEIL. Um…?

JESSE. Yes?

NEIL. Is there anything I should know?

JESSE. About?
NEIL. Black dick. About taking Black dick?
> *(Beat.)*

JESSE. Breathe.

9.

(Tribeca, April 2013. A bed. After sex.)

JESSE. I remember my parents gave me a box set of *The Cosby Show* before I left home for college. I wore that shit out.

NEIL. I fucking loved that show.

JESSE. Really?

NEIL. Yes, really. White people watched *The Cosby Show*.

JESSE. Yeah, I know that white people... That... That's not what I was...

> *(**NEIL** chuckles at **JESSE**'s inability to form a sentence.)*

Shut up.

(Beat.)

The thing is...the Huxtables? They looked like us. Like my family. I mean, my parents weren't doctors or lawyers, but they believed in education. They stressed the importance of discipline and hard work and... goodness, you know? In striving to be good. And I don't know... Somehow it became such a polarizing show. I mean, there are people who hate it. They say it's inauthentic. And white-washed. And maybe the show didn't liberate us. Maybe it wasn't the revolution we needed at the time, but for me...for me it was the first time I saw Black people who I could relate to in the mainstream media.

NEIL. That's not insignificant.

JESSE. No. And you know even if Bill Cosby turns out to have done a lot of shit things behind the scenes, which... I'm not condoning. At all. But I mean...does his behavior completely invalidate the show? Whatever good it did? Should it?

(Slight beat.)

NEIL. I had the biggest crush on Malcolm-Jamal Warner.

(**JESSE** *gives* **NEIL** *a look.*)

Don't give me that look. He was cute!

JESSE. Okay...

NEIL. Poor dyslexic Theo. I would've taught him to read.

(He looks at **JESSE.***)*

Among other things.

10.

(St. Paul, early April 2015. Phone call.)

NEIL. So, I mean, there's the Affordable Care Act, right? And the Lilly Ledbetter Fair Pay Act. And the repeal of "Don't Ask Don't Tell." And the end of the war in Iraq. And that's just for starters.

He's also smart and thoughtful and compassionate—

JESSE. And hot—

NEIL. Right and incredibly good looking. And his personal integrity is pretty much unimpeachable. AND he's married to Michelle, who is like, well, *everything*. And I know this goes without saying—

JESSE. But—

NEIL. But—ha—but the fact that he's African-American is a clear and decisive blow against four hundred plus years of slavery. I mean, the White House was built by Black men and women, most of whom were slaves.

Frederick Douglass and even Martin Luther King, Jr. were never even invited to sleep there, not even for one night even though they visited, and now, NOW, a Black man fucking LIVES there.

   (Slight beat.)

I honestly don't think I will ever see anything in my lifetime as significant as his election to the office of President. I just…

Like I think that that was pretty much the pinnacle, you know?

That was my political Mount Everest. It might be America's. You know, at least until Hillary wins next year.

(Slight beat.)

Wait, but sorry... You asked me a question before. It was...um...

Remind me?

JESSE. How's Baltimore?

11.

(JESSE speaks out.)

JESSE. I never learned to ride a bicycle. Given my balance struggles it always seemed too much of a risk. It's a huge regret of mine. "So learn now," you might say. "Now that yr grown, now that you KNOW what it is that ails you. It's never too late to learn something new." I find statements of that kind to be akin to the one that teachers are so fond of espousing. You must know it? It goes: There is no such thing as a dumb question.

I would assert that not only are there such things as dumb questions, but that there are such things as dumb statements.

I don't know who said it first. Who raised their hand at a gathering of educators and who when called upon stood up in the auditorium or assembly hall or wherever and proudly proclaimed that ALL QUESTIONS WERE VALID. That no child should EVER be made to feel less than brilliant even if their query CLEARLY called their mental faculties into question. I don't know who made sure that it was passed down from generation to generation. Who insisted that it be emblazoned on every educator's classroom wall. That it be a part of every educator's welcome to grade X speech, but it has persisted.

In my opinion—and it is humble, my opinion—that educator, that...person, should be shot. Or, at least, dragged behind something fast moving for an unspecified distance. Long enough to encourage them to recant. That seems a fitting punishment. To me at least.

(Beat.)

Anyway, I'm pretty sure that the statement has been proven false by now. That people generally acknowledge 'the fact' of dumb questions.

But if it hasn't—unequivocally—if any of you remain unconvinced, well then, there's nothing I can do to save you. You are stupid and you are going to die. And that is the long and the short of it. Oh, unless you are a teacher, a middle school teacher especially.

You will never die. You will live forever. You will make no money and suffer...rather like an artist. What is it they call them...starving?

You will always be hungry, but you will outlast us all. So...congratulations.

    (Beat.)

I couldn't teach. I don't know enough about anything. Not even myself.

12.

(St. Paul, November 24, 2014. A street.)

NEIL. Fuck!

JESSE. Breathe, Neil. / Just breathe.

NEIL. What the fuck!

JESSE. That's right. Get it ALL out. It's gonna be okay.

NEIL. How is this okay, huh? How the fuck / is this okay?

JESSE. Okay, that's not what I said. I didn't say it *was* okay. That what happened with Darren Wilson was okay. I said it will *be* okay / in the end.

NEIL. People are killing people and no one seems to care—

JESSE. Plenty of people care. You care, babe. You care. Come on now.

NEIL. I get scared for you.

JESSE. You... Sorry / what?

NEIL. When you go to the store or to the U for class or wherever. Every time you leave the house / I can't help panicking.

JESSE. Neil, what are you talking about?

NEIL. Trayvon was eating Skittles. Eric Garner had a pack of cigarettes. Tamir was holding a gun. / A toy gun!

JESSE. Neil...

NEIL. And they shot him. They put a bullet in his stomach before the squad car had even come to a complete stop. A twelve-year-old boy!

JESSE. Neil, I know. Yr lecturing—

NEIL. And now this fucking acquittal, which basically says that it's okay to shoot brown boys—

JESSE. Listen to me. Neil, listen. Nothing's going to happen to me at Whole Foods. It's Whole Foods.

NEIL. This isn't a joke, Jesse.

JESSE. I'm just pointing out that the likelihood of some horrible thing—

NEIL. Doesn't it freak you out?

JESSE. Doesn't / what?

NEIL. The fact that we're living in a world where not everyone AGREES with the statement "Black Lives Matter—"

JESSE. All lives matter / Neil—

NEIL. I KNOW THAT ALL LIVES—! That intrinsically—! Fuck, Jesse. How do you not—? Saying "All Lives Matter" is like running through a cancer fundraiser and saying "THERE'S OTHER DISEASES TOO."

JESSE. Neil—

NEIL. Look, you don't have to join the movement or whatever. You don't have to march or rally or call or write letters or even get fucking angry. I don't care about that. I don't. What I do care about is YOU. Is YR life. I want YOU to care, TOO—

JESSE. I do.

NEIL. Do you?

JESSE. Yes, of course, I do.

NEIL. Do you care about the fact that somewhere someone is celebrating the court's decision not to punish another white man for shooting a Black man? Do you understand that that poses a threat to YOU? To US? Do you get that? Because that's what—The fact that— I mean, doesn't that just—? Fuck, Jesse! Doesn't it make you just wanna—

JESSE. Kill someone?

(Slight beat.)

Yeah, Neil. It does.

13.

(Tribeca, February 2013. **JESSE** *puts on a song, something like Sam Cooke's* **["TWISTIN' THE NIGHT AWAY"]**.*)**

NEIL. Did I ever tell you that my grandparents saw Sam Cooke in concert?

JESSE. What? *No.*

NEIL. Yeah, this was back in the early sixties. Sixty-three maybe? And they were in Miami for New Year's or something and they heard that he was playing at this little club downtown so they went. Cause I mean he was famous at that point.

JESSE. He was a sensation.

NEIL. Right. And my grandma says that it was a little tense at first because they were some of the only white people there.

JESSE. "In a crowd of Negroes."

NEIL. Which they were totally cool with, jerk.

*(***JESSE** *smiles.)*

Anyway, my grandma says it was amazing. The best concert she's ever been to. I think he was shot soon after that.

---

* A license to produce THIS BITTER EARTH does not include a performance license for "TWISTIN THE NIGHT AWAY." The publisher and author suggest that the licensee contact ASCAP or BMI to ascertain the music publisher and contact such music publisher to license or acquire permission for performance of the song. If a license or permission is unattainable for "TWISTIN THE NIGHT AWAY," the licensee may not use the song in THIS BITTER EARTH but should create an original composition in a similar style or use a similar song in the public domain. For further information, please see Music Use Note on page 3.

JESSE. Wow.

NEIL. Yeah.

JESSE. How incredible. To be a part of history like that.

NEIL. We are a part of history like that.

(Slight beat.)

Hey.

JESSE. Hay is for horses, Neil.

*(**NEIL** extends his hand.)*

NEIL. Come on.

JESSE. Come on to where?

*(**NEIL** begins to do the twist.)*

Yeah, no. Contrary to popular belief, not all Black people like to dance.

NEIL. I'm not talking about all Black people, Jesse, I'm talking about you. And you *do* like to dance. You danced on our first date.

JESSE. First of all, it wasn't a date. And second, I only "danced" —if you can even call it that—because we were in a gay bar in the West Village and the playlist was fire.

NEIL. Yeah, well this is Sam Cooke and I want to see you move yr hips. Hand. Give it here.

JESSE. Neil…

NEIL. For once in yr life just…say…yes.

*(A moment and then **JESSE** accepts **NEIL**'s offered hand.)*

JESSE. Yr annoying as hell, you know that?

NEIL. I do. Now twist.

*(**JESSE** does. Hesitantly, at first, and then with more enthusiasm.)*

See, this isn't so bad.

JESSE. Maybe not for you.

NEIL. You know, you pretend to be a Grinch, but you suck at it.

JESSE. Whatever.

(They continue to dance. NEIL has an idea.)

NEIL. Hey.

JESSE. What now?

NEIL. Yell.

JESSE. Um…excuse / me—?

NEIL. Yell! Throw yr head back and—

(NEIL yells. JESSE attempts to quiet him.)

JESSE. Neil, are you crazy? The neighbors will hear / you—

NEIL. So the fuck what?

JESSE. So I'd like to not be kicked out of this building!

NEIL. It's cathartic.

JESSE. I don't need catharsis.

NEIL. Of all the people I know you are the one most in need of catharsis.

Come on. Try it.

JESSE. No.

NEIL. For me?

JESSE. What part of "no" do you not understand?

(NEIL twists JESSE's nipple. JESSE yells.)

OW! FUCK, THAT'S MY NIPPLE, YOU ASSHOLE!

(NEIL smiles.)

NEIL. Well, that's a start.

14.

(St. Paul, September 2015.)

JESSE. I mean, Black feminism, right? Audre Lorde. Kimberlé Crenshaw. And the whole "personal is political" thing. And like, contact hypothesis, you know? The idea that intergroup contact can effectively reduce prejudice between majority and minority group members? Like whites and Blacks? Or straights and gays? Like…okay, take gay marriage, which—

NEIL. We're not discussing—

JESSE. We're not discussing, right—

NEIL. Even though we've been together for three years—

JESSE. But like the brilliance of the campaign was its simplicity.

NEIL. And there it is… / the wall.

JESSE. What turned the tide? Gay people coming out to their straight friends. That personal connection. That realization that homos were people, too. *That* influenced their thinking and thus their vote. And don't think I didn't hear you because I did hear you, but I'm choosing to ignore you, because I'm in the middle of making a point, which is that THAT is why today in America same-sex couples have the fundamental right to marry on the same terms as opposite-sex couples. Because of fucking Black feminism.

15.

(St. Paul, September 2014. An apartment. **NEIL** *enters with a duffel.)*

NEIL. Hey.

    *(**JESSE** looks up.)*

JESSE. Hey, yr back. How was it?

NEIL. Sad. It was really fucking sad.

JESSE. I've been watching the news.

NEIL. It doesn't even begin to... I mean, maybe the BBC's getting it right? Or NPR? But CNN? Fucking Fox? There are too many agendas at play to get to any kind of real truth.

JESSE. Yeah, well they say it's relative. Truth.

NEIL. Yeah...

JESSE. What did they end up having you do?

NEIL. A lot actually. Cataloguing incoming donations. Distributing food. Water. The first day we got there a bunch of us marched down to the police station. And we got there and there was this row of uniformed officers, all of them white, and they were standing there, hands on their hips, arms crossed like... I don't know...like they were just waiting for us to wear ourselves out. And I kept thinking: How can they be so unfazed, you know? Like how can this be just another day on the job?

JESSE. Did you leave things better than you found them?

NEIL. Maybe? I think so. We tried.

JESSE. Good. That's good.

NEIL. But who really knows, you know?

    (Beat.)

JESSE. Are you hungry? I could make you a sandwich or something?

NEIL. No, I'm... We ate on the road.

JESSE. You sure?

NEIL. Yeah, thanks.

> *(Beat.)*

It was weird. Being there. It was good, obviously. Obviously, it was good, but also...weird. It's just I've never...

JESSE. You've never what?

NEIL. Felt so white.

> *(**JESSE** laughs.)*

It's not funny.

JESSE. Babe, you are so white.

NEIL. I know, okay, I know, I just... It's just that I've never had to prove myself before, you know? I've never had to somehow work to dispel the thought that I'm some kind of interloper. Some kind of spy.

JESSE. Welcome to my world.

> *(Beat.)*

NEIL. The thing is, I'm aware that on paper I have more in common with...well, you know, with those officers. But that's not who I am. That's not who I am.

> *(Beat.)*

Fuck, I'm tired. That drive's no joke.

> *(Beat.)*

I got yr messages. I'm sorry I didn't call back.

JESSE. You were busy. We were angry.

NEIL. I didn't know what to say. The whole trip I didn't know what to say.

JESSE. And now?

NEIL. And now I think... I think that you should be you and I should be me and we'll just...fill in the gaps for each other. We'll fill in the gaps. I think that's the only way this is gonna work.

JESSE. Deal.

> *(JESSE extends his hand. NEIL takes it. He pulls JESSE into an embrace.)*

I'm sorry.

NEIL. Me too.

> *(Beat.)*

You wanna tell me how rehearsals are going?

> *(NEIL begins to undress.)*

Preferably in the bedroom? Preferably naked?

> *(NEIL removes the last of his clothing. He tosses the item to JESSE, who catches it.)*

16.

*(**JESSE** speaks out.)*

JESSE. When I was a kid I believed in a great many things. The Bogeyman. Unspecified monsters in my closet, under my bed. Gryphons and jabberwocks. Flying monkeys and unicorns. The Tooth Fairy and Santa Claus. Now I find that even the most basic things stretch credibility.

Debt-free living, for example. The IRS. The Electoral College. I sometimes wonder if kindness really exists. And charity and hope and love. God. And creation and evolution. And all the science behind basic things like walking. Celsius. And centrifugal force and gravity.

I'm not so sure that I believe in gravity, though I've been told again and again, by people who I suppose would know, that it exists.

(Slight beat.)

Or God. Did I say God already?

17.

(St. Paul, June 2015. **NEIL** *is on his computer.)*

NEIL. Oh my God.

(Beat.)

Oh my God.

(Beat.)

Oh my fucking God!

JESSE. Will you please turn that off and come to bed?

NEIL. I can't. It's like heroin. Or coke. I can't stop watching. Everything about him is just so…odious. His face. His hair. His stupid red tie.

JESSE. Neil—

NEIL. And the things he says. God! It's like… It's like the second coming of Jerry Falwell.

JESSE. Please don't say that name in our apartment.

NEIL. Or Roy Cohn.

JESSE. Or that one.

NEIL. Or Hitler.

JESSE. Neil, please—

NEIL. Or that governor from Alaska. / What was her name? Jesse, what was the name of the woman from Alaska who ran for President?

JESSE. No. I will not say her name. I will not. It was Vice President, actually, and I will not say her name.

*(***NEIL** *remembers.)*

NEIL. Sarah Palin!

JESSE. I'm going to kill you.

NEIL. Sarah fucking Palin.

18.

(Tribeca, April 2012. An apartment. **JESSE** *is on his computer.* **NEIL** *watches* **JESSE**.*)*

JESSE. I can feel yr eyes…

NEIL. Sorry.

(Beat.)

JESSE. Neil.

NEIL. What? I'm just sitting here.

JESSE. Staring. Yr staring and staring is creepy. I can't write if you / stare—

NEIL. Okay! I know. Okay.

(Beat.)

How's that fingernail taste, by the way?

JESSE. How's the what?

NEIL. Never mind.

JESSE. Read yr book!

NEIL. Fine!

(Beat.)

JESSE. Oh my God / Neil!

NEIL. Sorry, sorry! It's just—

JESSE. What? It's just what—?

NEIL. Can I read it?

JESSE. Can you…?

NEIL. Whatever yr…?

(Slight beat.)

It's just…yr always writing. And I've never really… I mean, you've talked about yr various projects, about yr process, but I… I haven't actually read yr work.

I feel like I have. I feel like I'd know it if I encountered it somewhere, but I'm missing something. A huge part of who you are. And that feels... Will you read me a section? Rough or unfinished or whatever. Just something? Please.

*(A moment and then **JESSE** relents.)*

JESSE. Fine.

(He takes a breath and begins to read.)

"In my dream, though admittedly it was more like Dorothy's than like Martin's, there were no white people or children. There were no munchkins or fields of poppies. No 'bad news.' And no 'easing on down' of any yellow brick roads. It was decidedly adult, my dream, though not pornographic, as you might assume. In the dream I was at a party in a penthouse somewhere and everyone was Black. From darkest night to caramel to white chocolate. Every shade and hue. Size and shape. The variety! THE HAIR! And EVERYONE was in costume! Lorraine was dressed as Josephine Baker. Ralph Ellison as Alex Haley. Even Langston, beautiful, elusive, ephemeral Langston, was present and accounted for and dressed as Gregory Hines! Queen Latifah was there dressed as you know who. And dear Jimmy Baldwin, who I've always had a little crush on, was there holding court in the entryway. Althea Gibson was there. And Ossie Davis and Ruby Dee. Alvin Ailey was two stepping with Maya Angelou. Louie and Marian were trading scats. Basquiat and Romare were talking technique. And Zora was taking drink orders! Everyone was living! Everyone was fabulous!

And I made my way through the various rooms, each strewn with more streamers and balloons than the last. A band played somewhere, my mother's favorite song, 'Boogie Wonderland.' And the people were getting down. You know the way we do. Like... DOWN!

I pushed my way through, every floor a dance floor. I stepped over Toussaint L'Ouverture who had literally hit the deck. I kissed Butterfly McQueen on the cheek. And then I turned a corner and found myself on a balcony overlooking, well, nothing. Nothing but space and silence.

And then...

"It's something, isn't it?" That voice. Soft. Caressing. I knew that voice. I turned. It was Essex Hemphill, legs crossed at the knee, a Tupac Shakur mask in his lap, a brown drink in his hand.

"It's quite the view," he said.

"Yes," I replied, "it is."

He joined me at the railing. He smelled of bourbon and something else.

Something sweet.

He said, "I have yet to understand why emotional expression by men must be understated or under control when the process of living requires the capacity to feel and express."

I looked over at him and I fell into his eyes. "I don't get it either," I said. And then he smiled and began to lean towards me. And I wondered, what's going to happen? Will we kiss? Oh God, will we kiss?

But no. Alas, he paused. His mouth brushed against my ear and he whispered gently, 'nice costume.'

And then I woke up.

> (**JESSE** *looks up from his computer. A moment and then* **NEIL** *moves to him and kisses his cheek.*)

19.

(Union Square, March 2012.)

NEIL. I don't even remember how I ended up with the megaphone in the first place. I mean, there were so many people and everyone was pressing in like… And at one point I looked down. Just like… And there it was in my hand.

JESSE. My roommate Rashaad was like, "are you coming to the march?" And I was like, "the march?" And he gave me a look like, really motherfucker? "Yeah, the Million Hoodie March. For Trayvon fucking Martin!" And clearly my face didn't make the right face because he followed it up with, "a seventeen-year-old Black boy gets shot on a city street in the so-called land of the free and the home of the brave and YR GONNA SIT IT OUT because you don't think it has anything to do with you?"

I still didn't make the right face. "Nah, nigga," he said, "we're going downtown!" And then he literally grabbed me and pulled me toward the door. "Hold up, hold up," I said, unfastening his fingers from my arm. "Rashaad, man. I have a thesis to write." And he said, "Jesse, man. You ain't writing yr thesis. Yr dicking around."

NEIL. And it wasn't like I had any intention of using it. Because I mean, number one: It wasn't mine, right? The megaphone. Not mine.

And number two: I was just there to support, you know? In solidarity.

But then the guy next to me noticed that I had it and he was like, "why the fuck aren't you using that thing?" And I was like…that's a good fucking question…

JESSE. We pushed our way to the park at Broadway and Fourteenth and the first thing I saw was this white boy climbing up on the statue of George Washington. And I'm thinking, he's the one with the bullhorn? He's the one hyping the crowd? This white guy? Please! We might all be Trayvon Martin, but honey we aren't all of us Black.

NEIL. So then, all of a sudden, I'm being hoisted up onto the statue.

You know the big statute of George Washington on his horse? Yeah, well I'm literally being pushed into his bronzed junk and I'm trying like hell to hold onto the megaphone with one hand and to stabilize myself with the other. And the people below me are like, "All right, white boy. Let's hear it." And I'm wracking my brain, you know? Like seriously stressing about what to say because the last thing that this crowd needs to hear is another empathetic white person talking about "I feel yr pain." And the first thing that pops into my head is this Essex Hemphill poem I'd memorized for a Queer Lit class my junior year of college.

JESSE. And this bitch, this bitch with the bullhorn, starts reciting "For My Own Protection". For My Own Fucking Protection! And I'm like, "Here we go again." Yet another example of blatant cultural appropriation. And I'm pissed, right? I'm pissed cause, what the fuck. And I'm looking around to see if anyone else is hearing what I'm hearing, feeling what I'm feeling, and I notice... I notice, and I'm shocked by this, I notice that the people are listening. That the people are nodding and "mm-hm-ing" and "amen-ing." The people are listening to the words of a virtually unknown Black queer poet GENIUS and they get it. They fucking get it. And before I even realize it I'm speaking the words along with him. Speaking Essex's life-saving words along with the white man with the bullhorn dangling from the statue.

The lives of Black men are priceless and can be saved, indeed!

*(St. Paul, early December 2015. A street. Suddenly, **NEIL**'s arms are around **JESSE**'s waist.)*

NEIL. Wait, wait, wait! How does it go again—?

JESSE. How do you not know this song? It's like essential—

NEIL. Essentially what? / And essential to whom—?

JESSE. What do you mean essentially what? / A proper education. A *basic* education—

NEIL. "Alabama, Alaska, Arizona, Arkansas…" / What comes after Arkansas—?

JESSE. I can't believe you went to private school—

NEIL. California! / "California—"

JESSE. Celia and Markus paid like forty thousand dollars a year for twelve years and you don't know what comes after Arkansas?

*(**JESSE** slips on a patch of ice. **NEIL** catches him.)*

NEIL. Whoa there, Tiger!

*(**JESSE** begins to laugh and then **NEIL** joins.)*

What are we laughing about?

JESSE. You just called me Tiger—!

NEIL. Why the fuck would I call you Tiger?

JESSE. No fucking clue!

*(**JESSE** slips again. Both men react.)*

JESSE.	NEIL.
Shit! This fucking sidewalk!	WHOA! Watch it—!

NEIL. *(Continued.)* The last thing we need is a broken ankle—

JESSE. Yeah, or a broken butt!

(They both find the prospect of a broken butt hilarious.)

NEIL. We definitely do not need a broken butt. I like yr butt the way it is.

JESSE. "Iowa, Kansas, Kentucky, Louisiana, Maine..."

*(**NEIL** joins.)*

JESSE/NEIL. "Maryland, Massachusetts, Michigan—"

*(The sound of breaking glass and then— **NEIL** is gone. St. Paul, mid-December 2015. Eventually—.)*

JESSE. We were almost to the corner. Maybe fifty feet from the entrance to the bar. Neil was holding me. We were singing and laughing and the bottle... The bottle came out of nowhere. It was full. When it broke against his head it was... And then he fell. Neil, he...sank to the sidewalk. His whole body. The whole weight of his body suddenly on me, pulling me down with him. Pulling me down to the sidewalk with the bottle and the beer. There was beer everywhere. And the blood, gushing from his head.

(Slight beat.)

And I tried to...um... I tried to...

(Beat.)

I remember the blood. I can still see the blood.

20.

(St. Paul, October 2014. An apartment.)

NEIL. I don't believe you.

JESSE. What? What did I / do?

NEIL. You didn't even try. My friends were here in our living room and you couldn't even bother to say hello.

JESSE. I'm sorry, okay. I had a long day. It's midterms and my students are freaking out and I forgot / that yr committee was gonna be here.

NEIL. I asked you weeks ago if I could host. Weeks. Because I know how you feel about Black Lives Matter. How uncomfortable / it makes you.

JESSE. It doesn't make / me uncomfortable.

NEIL. Bullshit.

JESSE. What?

NEIL. You heard me. Bullshit. And the fact that you feel the need to so vehemently refute my assessment of your comfort level is proof of how uncomfortable BLM makes you.

(Beat.)

My friends were really excited to meet you. I've told them all about you.

JESSE. Yeah, well I didn't ask you to do that.

NEIL. Yr my boyfriend, Jesse. I'm gonna talk about you with my friends. / That's what boyfriends do!

JESSE. All right. Okay!

NEIL. Do you not talk about me with your friends?

JESSE. That's not what I'm saying.

NEIL. Oh, no? Then please enlighten me.

JESSE. I just don't think you have to get all—
NEIL. What? Worked up? LOUD?

>   (**JESSE** *shushes* **NEIL.**)

Yr unbelievable, you know that? / Truly unbelievable—

JESSE. Listen, I'm sorry I didn't stay for the meeting. It was super sweet of the group to invite me to join. I just... wasn't in the mood.

NEIL. You never are.

>   (*Beat.*)

Yr a fucking double minority, Jesse.

JESSE. What does that have to do with / anything?

NEIL. Yr Black and yr gay and yr educated and yr passionate and yr talented as fuck and it's 2014 and people like you, people who look like you, are being killed, and yr just standing there. Yr just standing there. Doing nothing.

JESSE. I'm not doing nothing.

>   (**NEIL** *gives* **JESSE** *a look.*)

I'm living my life, Neil. I'm living my fucking life. What else do you want from me?

NEIL. More, okay? I want fucking more.

JESSE. Yeah, well this is what I have to give. If you don't like it...

>   (**JESSE** *doesn't finish his sentence.*)

NEIL. If I don't like it what, huh? What?

>   (*Beat.*)

Are you breaking up with me?

JESSE. I didn't say that.

NEIL. You didn't SAY anything!

>   (*Beat.*)

Jesse!

JESSE. Don't you get tired of this?

NEIL. This? What is this?

JESSE. All this talk. This constant nitpicky back and forth bullshit. Yr this way. I'm that way. Change, change, change.

NEIL. I'm not trying to change you.

    *(**JESSE** gives **NEIL** a look.)*

What, I'm not. I wouldn't. That's not what I... You can't think that's what I want. I love you.

    (Slight beat.)

Don't you know that?

21.

(West Village. April 2012. A diner.)

JESSE. You seriously want to talk about my thesis?

NEIL. Sure, why not?

JESSE. Because it's boring / that's why not.

NEIL. It's not boring.

JESSE. Trust me, it is.

NEIL. It's yr thesis.

JESSE. Even to me. Especially / to me—

NEIL. So then bore me. Put me to sleep. I dare you.

(Slight beat.)

JESSE. Fine. I'm writing a play. The end.

NEIL. Nah, yr not getting off that easy. Tell me more. What's it about?

*(**JESSE** smiles.)*

JESSE. Essex Hemphill, actually. The poet you quoted / at the rally—

NEIL. At the rally? No way!

JESSE. Yes, way.

NEIL. Well that's…weird.

JESSE. I thought so, too.

NEIL. And it's about his life or…?

JESSE. It's less about him in a biographical sense and more inspired by him. By his work. It's a kind of meditation on blackness and queerness and neuroses and…

NEIL. And what? Well, don't stop now.

JESSE. So… I feel like before we go any further with this conversation…you should know that I'm—

NEIL. What? Canadian?

(A shared smile.)

JESSE. I just feel like it would be irresponsible of me not to mention the fact that I've made all the wrong decisions in my life. Like all the mistakes. From getting an MFA at an outrageously expensive institution when I have like fifty cents in my bank account to cracking inappropriate jokes with cute guys I stalked on Facebook then messaged and who for some reason said yes to meeting up for coffee.

NEIL. You think I'm cute?

JESSE. You know you are.

*(**NEIL** leans in.)*

NEIL. So…if you were gonna grab a drink somewhere in the neighborhood. Something not coffee…where would you go?

JESSE. Where would I…? Are you serious?

NEIL. Yes, I'm serious.

JESSE. You aren't sick of me yet?

NEIL. Why would I be sick of you?

JESSE. Because people get sick of other people! Because people tend to get very sick of me VERY quickly. And besides my drinking usually leads to…

NEIL. What? What does drinking usually lead to?

*(**JESSE** doesn't respond.)*

Now yr shy?

JESSE. When I drink I get…loud.

NEIL. You mean, loud-er?

JESSE. HA. HA. NO. Opinionated. I get opinionated. Bitch.

*(**NEIL** playfully shoves **JESSE**. **JESSE** playfully shoves him back.)*

NEIL. So where to next?

22.

(JESSE speaks out.)

JESSE. The first boy I ever liked was white. We were in the second grade and he had a mullet and a huge gap between his front two teeth. I didn't know I was gay then. I mean, if someone had called me that, "gay," I wouldn't have known what they meant. All I knew then was that I liked that boy.

The first boy I ever kissed was white. The first boy I had sex with was white. My first serious boyfriend was white. The first boy I moved in with was white. My first meet the parents' moment. My first knock-down, drag-out fight. My first HIV scare. All white. White, white, white, white, white. And then there's Neil...

(Beat.)

And it's not that I don't like Black men, or non-white men for that matter, I do. I mean, I like men. Period. But... See, the thing is, it's not even a preference, really. White men over... It's that Black men just don't like me. They don't get me. And frankly, frankly, I don't get them either. All the posturing. And the posing. And the hyper-masculinity. And yes, I realize that I'm that dipping into some pretty dangerous territory here. That I'm lumping an entire group of people together based on my experiences with a select few so... But I mean we all do it, right? Lump?

And maybe it's that white men are allowed to be soft. That they're encouraged by their mothers or their grandmothers or whomever to be artistic and self-aware and gentle. And maybe Black men aren't given that opportunity, not with the same frequency anyway, because maybe gentle gets you killed.

And maybe I'm attracted to that softness.

And maybe growing up in Kansas surrounded by white people, by white culture—whatever that is—and feeling the need to be good and to play nice and to make myself palatable and unobtrusive, you know? Lowering my...

> *(Slight beat.)*

My...

> *(Beat.)*

Anyway.

23.

(St. Paul, late April 2015. An apartment.)

JESSE. Get out.

NEIL. Jesse—

JESSE. I said, GET OUT. / GET THE FUCK OUT!

NEIL. I CAN EXPLAIN. / PLEASE LET ME TRY TO EXPLAIN!

JESSE. What makes you think we have the kind of relationship where you can say to me I FUCKED someone else and then we can have a reasonable conversation about it?

NEIL. Babe / please.

JESSE. FUCK YOU!

NEIL. Jesse.

JESSE. Say my name one more time and I will kill you. I will fucking strangle you with my bare hands.

NEIL. It didn't mean anything. / I promise it didn't mean anything!

JESSE. AND THAT'S SUPPOSED TO MAKE IT BETTER?

NEIL. NO! I DON'T KNOW!

JESSE. YOU DON'T / KNOW?

NEIL. IT WAS AFTER THE RIOT.[*]

It was after the riot and everything was... I mean, it was crazy. The march from City Hall to Inner Harbor had been peaceful. And then someone threw a rock at a cop and then another at a squad car and then a storefront window shattered and all hell broke loose and all of us,

---

[*] The Baltimore Riots (April 18, 2015 – May 3, 2015) began after the death of Freddie Gray in police custody.

the volunteers, were like, what the fuck? What the fuck are we supposed to / do?

JESSE. So you fucked someone? Someone threw a rock and things got crazy and the only thing you could think to do was to fuck / someone?

NEIL. I was stupid. I was stupid and I'm sorry!

(Beat.)

JESSE. Who was he?

NEIL. What?

JESSE. Who was he? The guy? Who was the guy?

NEIL. I—

JESSE. Yr so sorry? Yr so full of regret?

NEIL. Jesse, I—

JESSE. Then tell me. Tell me his name. First. And last. Did you get that far? Did you exchange middle names? What about occupations? What does he do? Where is he from? Does he have brothers and sisters? Does he like his parents? Are his grandparents still alive? What's his favorite color? Favorite movie? Favorite book? Is he right or left-handed? Does he prefer Disney World or Disney Land? Cats or dogs? Coffee or tea? Does he want children? Was his dick bigger than mine? Was he white? Huh, Neil? Was he white? Was he? Neil, was he?

(Beat.)

NEIL. Yes.

*(A long moment and then **JESSE** throws himself at **NEIL**. They struggle. **JESSE** lands a punch.)*

OW! FUCK!

*(**NEIL** holds his face.)*

I'm fucking bleeding!

*(**JESSE** pulls away from **NEIL**.)*

JESSE. Go.

NEIL. Jesse, I—

JESSE. I said, go.
NEIL. I'm so sorry.
JESSE. Get out!
NEIL. Please!
JESSE. Get the fuck out!
NEIL. I love you, Jesse. I do. I love you.
JESSE. GET THE FUCK OUT, YOU STUPID FUCK!

(A long moment. Finally, **NEIL** *exits.)*

24.

(St. Paul, early May 2015. **JESSE** *moves to his laptop and begins to type. He considers. Deletes. Re-types. Re-reads – his lips moving, but no sound. A phone begins to ring. His phone.* **JESSE** *turns down the volume of the music and checks the number. He considers. Then doesn't answer.* **NEIL** *appears. He leaves a message.)*

NEIL. Hi, it's me. Look, I know you don't want to talk to me right now. Or, ever again, maybe, and I get that. I hate it. I fucking hate that that's maybe true…but I understand. What I did…um…what I did was… I need you to know that I've never been sorrier about anything else in my life. Please, know that I…

(Beat.)

Um… I keep thinking about this one day, it was about a year ago, and we were holding hands because that's what we used to do when we were together, hold hands, and this guy, this nice-looking, put-together white guy, passed us. Passed you. And he said, and I'll never forget this, he said, "you fucking n-word faggot." Like he was saying "good afternoon" or "nice shirt," you know? With a smile on his face. And I remember I stopped, right there in the middle of the sidewalk, and I was ready to beat the shit out of him, out of that smug, probably closeted, gay motherfucker on the corner of Hennepin and Lake. Or, at least, ask him where the fuck he got off saying bullshit like that, but you… You were like, "it's not worth it." I remember you gripped my arm and you said, "Leave it alone." And I did. I turned back around and you re-took my hand and we kept right on walking like nothing had happened. Only something did happen. That was the beginning of everything. The moment everything... Because the thing is, Jesse, ever since that day, I've felt the same feeling. The feeling I felt when that fucker said what he said to you, the love of my life. Still. Ever since that day I've felt like fucking shit up.

*(***NEIL** *hangs up the phone.)*

25.

*(**JESSE** speaks out.)*

JESSE. Belief in anything... In the Electoral College or the IRS. In another human. Or in God. Requires faith. A kind of combination cliff dive, trapeze act without a net, without knowledge of the exact depth of the water below. One wonders, will I break my neck? Will he break my heart? And if I break...will I survive?

26.

(West Village, April 2012. A gay bar. Music*. Lights. They might have to yell.)

NEIL. So...this is yr spot. I like it. It's got character. It's that good kind of seedy.

(JESSE laughs.)

What? What did I say?

JESSE. "That good kind of seedy?" Who are you?

NEIL. You know what I mean. It's divey. Rough around the edges, but in a good way. Hey, be nice / to me.

JESSE. I am nice. I'm the nicest person I know.

NEIL. Yeah, you just keep telling yrself that.

(A shared smile.)

You know, I've walked down Christopher Street a million times and I've never noticed this place.

JESSE. You've seen it. You just haven't stopped. White guys rarely do.

NEIL. Hey, I don't discriminate. As long as the drinks are strong, and the men are hot, I'm game.

JESSE. Is that right?

NEIL. Fuck, yeah.

(JESSE laughs.)

So why is this yr favorite?

JESSE. Honestly? I like that it's brown. That the patrons, by and large, are brown. Which is funny because ordinarily

---

* A license to produce THIS BITTER EARTH does not include a performance license for any third-party or copyrighted music. Licensees should create an original composition or use music in the public domain. For further information, please see Music Use Note on page 3.

that wouldn't be something that would matter to me, that my gay space also be a brown space, but when I first moved to the city I didn't feel welcome in Chelsea or in the East Village—

NEIL. Who does?

JESSE. Right, yeah, well a boyfriend introduced me to this place. After we broke-up I used to come here three, four times a week. Sit at the bar. Have a drink or six. I made friends with the bartenders. The regulars.

NEIL. It's yr *Cheers*.

JESSE. It's my *Cheers*.

> *(A shared smile. And then—A gay club hit begins to play.*)*

NEIL.	**JESSE.**
OH MY GOD,	OH MY GOD,
I FUCKING LOVE THIS SONG!	I LOVE THIS FUCKING SONG!

> *(The men begin to sing along at the top of their lungs. At some point during the song, **NEIL** grabs **JESSE** and kisses him. They move to the bed. Clothes are removed.)*

---

* A license to produce THIS BITTER EARTH does not include a performance license for any third-party or copyrighted music. Licensees should create an original composition or use music in the public domain. For further information, please see Music Use Note on page 3.

27.

(St. Paul, November 2015. An apartment. After a failed attempt at sex.)

NEIL. I don't...um...sorry, I don't know what's wrong / with me.

JESSE. It's okay.

NEIL. Yeah, I'm gonna have to disagree with you.

JESSE. It happens.

NEIL. Not to me. I mean, I know that guys say that. That they say, "I swear this has never happened to me before," but I swear this has never happened to me / before.

JESSE. It's fine, Neil. Really. I should be writing anyway.

NEIL. Jesse.

JESSE. What?

(NEIL gestures. He doesn't have words.)

Yr putting too much pressure on the moment. You don't have to impress me.

NEIL. I *want* to impress you. I want to impress upon you the depth of my commitment to you.

JESSE. You don't need yr dick for that.

(Beat.)

NEIL. We could do other things...

JESSE. I'm not really in the mood anymore. Sorry, I just...

NEIL. No, it's... Yr right. I'm trying too hard. I pressurized the situation.

JESSE. This isn't a "situation."

NEIL. Yeah, well it feels like a situation to me. I feel like I'm drowning in a fucking / situation.

JESSE. Hey, stop it. We hit a bump in the road and we repaired the damage.

Let's not blow one ineffectual attempt at intimacy out of proportion.

We're good.

NEIL. You promise?

JESSE. I do.

> (**NEIL** *is still sullen.*)

I love you.

NEIL. I love you, too.

> (**JESSE** *kisses* **NEIL** *on the cheek.*)

JESSE. Now go put on some fucking pants!

> (**JESSE** *playfully swats* **NEIL**'s *ass and moves to his computer.* **NEIL** *checks his phone.*)

NEIL. Shit.

JESSE. What? What is it?

NEIL. Nothing. Sorry, it's nothing…

JESSE. Yr face doesn't look like nothing. What's going on?

> (**NEIL** *offers his phone.* **JESSE** *reads.*)

Fuck. This is…? This happened today?

NEIL. Yeah.

JESSE. Is he dead?[*]

NEIL. The article doesn't say.

> *(Beat.)*

JESSE. You should go.

NEIL. What?

JESSE. I'm sure BLM is rallying the troops as we speak. You should be there.

NEIL. Jesse.

---

[*] Jamar Clark, a 24-year-old Black man, was shot by Minneapolis police on November 15, 2015. Clark died the next day.

JESSE. Neil, the Minneapolis police just shot an unarmed Black man less than twenty miles from our apartment. Go.

> *(More hesitation.)*

For real, go.

> *(**NEIL** begins to pull on clothes.)*

NEIL. Yr sure about this? Cause I don't have to go. You and me and Black Lives Matter don't exactly have the best track record—

JESSE. What have you said to me time and time again, huh? "When the shit hits the fan, that's when the movement needs its allies most."

NEIL. You were listening.

JESSE. Of course I was listening.

> *(Slight beat.)*

Wear a hat. It's cold out there.

> *(**NEIL** moves to exit.)*

Oh, and Neil?

> *(**NEIL** turns back.)*

If something goes down. Like if something really bad / goes down...

NEIL. I'll call. I promise. I'll call.

> *(**NEIL** exits. **JESSE** moves to his computer. He types, searching for information. Eventually, he reads.)*

JESSE. "Police said that at some point during the struggle an officer fired at least once, hitting the man. Witnesses said that Clark was handcuffed when he was shot." Jesus.

> *(**JESSE** closes the monitor. A moment and then he begins to pull on clothes. He grabs his coat and leaves the apartment.)*

28.

(NEIL speaks out.)

NEIL. It's the little things. It's the way he fills the ice cube tray one little rectangle at a time. It's the way his pockets are always full of paper. Post-its. Napkins. Receipts. All of them covered in illegible scrawl. It's the way that every part of his body is ticklish during sex. Literally every part. It's the way he sometimes lets go of my hand when we're in public because he knows something that I don't, senses a danger that I'm oblivious to. It's the way he sometimes has to flag down bartenders to get a drink even if the bar is empty. It's the way that as soon as I arrive we couldn't get better service. It's the way he smiles in the face of bullshit like that. The way he holds his head high and squares his shoulders as if to say, "Adversity? Ha!"

It's the way that history isn't history at all. Or, at least, the way that it doesn't stay in the past. The way that the past fucks the present. And the way that Jesse gets that, understands that, and still gets out of bed in the morning and makes coffee. It's the way that there will always be things I don't fully understand. Things I don't see. Or hear. It's the way that my privilege is inescapable. The way that no matter what I do, no matter how many rallies or protests I attend to stand in solidarity with the violated, with the hurting, this...

(NEIL indicates his skin.)

Is my reality. It's the way that he loves me in spite of my reality.

(Beat.)

It's the way I catch him looking at me sometimes. Looking at me like, "Yeah."

>   *(Beat.)*

It's the little things.

29.

(St. Paul, June 2015. An apartment.)

NEIL. Ok, so I'm here. What do you want?

> *(Beat.)*

Jesse?

> *(Beat.)*

Shit, *you* texted *me*. You texted and I dropped what I was doing and high-tailed it over here to the apartment that used to be our apartment, which is fucking weird. Which *feels* fucking weird, using my fob and my key to enter the apartment that is no longer mine. You called and I came.

> *(Beat.)*

Jesse, what the fuck?

JESSE. Did you hear about the guy in Charleston?[*]

He shot up a Black church. Motherfucker killed nine people last night.

Nine Black people at a fucking prayer meeting.

NEIL. Is that why you asked me here? / To talk about Charleston?

JESSE. They let him in. I can't get over that. They welcomed him into their space. They embraced him. Loved him in that Christian way. They were concerned for his soul and he shot them! I mean, what the fuck? And you know the other thing I can't... The other thing that

---

[*] On the evening of June 17, 2015, Dylann Roof, a 21-year-old white supremacist, murdered nine Black Americans during a prayer service at the Emanuel African Methodist Church in downtown Charleston, South Carolina.

makes absolutely no sense to me... The photos. Have you seen them? They're still praying. Heads bowed. Hands clasped. They invite this man into their church. He kills them. Feels justified in killing them. And what do they do? They fucking pray.

NEIL. We all deal with loss in different ways.

JESSE. This isn't loss, Neil. This is murder. Nobody should have to deal with murder. Prayer shouldn't be our only recourse.

NEIL. I know.

> *(Beat.)*

JESSE. I started a new play. It's a one-man show. This guy. "No name." Black. Thirties. He addresses the audience. He informs them that he is dying. Guess what from?

NEIL. You know I'm crap at guessing / games—

JESSE. Just guess!

NEIL. I don't know.

JESSE. Blackness. He's dying of blackness. Isn't that fucking hilarious?

> *(Beat.)*

NEIL. Jesse, why did you call me over here?
Jesse.

JESSE. Come home.

> *(Slight beat.)*

I want you to come home. Fuck what happened in Baltimore. Fuck Jamie or Jasper or whatever the fuck his fucking name was. Fuck all the shit that happened / in the past.

NEIL. Babe.

JESSE. Fuck it! People are being killed in churches. In fucking pews, Neil. And prayers don't stop bullets. Please just...come home.

> *(Beat.)*

Please...

NEIL. Yeah. Okay.
>   *(**NEIL** takes **JESSE**'s hand.)*

I will.

31.

>(**JESSE** *speaks out.*)

JESSE. They asked me to speak at his funeral. Neil's parents. They asked and I said yes because how could I not?

>(*Beat.*)

We'd never discussed death. Dying. Not in any concrete way anyway. It never seemed…appropriate, given how alive we were. And no, the irony of that statement is not lost on me.

>(*St. Paul, early December 2015. A street. Suddenly,* **NEIL**'s *arms are around* **JESSE**'s *waist.*)

NEIL. Wait, wait, wait! How does it go again—?

JESSE. How do you not know this song? It's like essential—

NEIL. Essentially what? / And essential to whom—?

JESSE. What do you mean essentially what? / A proper education. A basic education—

NEIL. "Alabama, Alaska, Arizona, Arkansas…" / What comes after Arkansas—?

JESSE. I can't believe you went to private school—

NEIL. California! / "California—"

JESSE. Celia and Markus paid like forty thousand dollars a year for twelve years and you don't know what comes after Arkansas—?

>(**JESSE** *slips on a patch of ice.* **NEIL** *catches him.*)

NEIL. Whoa there, Tiger!

>(**JESSE** *begins to laugh and then* **NEIL** *joins.*)

What are we laughing about?

JESSE. You just called me Tiger!

NEIL. Why the fuck would I call you Tiger?

JESSE. No fucking clue!

(JESSE slips again. Both men react.)

JESSE.	**NEIL**.
Shit! This fucking sidewalk!	WHOA! Watch it—!

NEIL. *(Continued.)* The last thing we need is a broken ankle—

JESSE. Yeah, or a broken butt!

(They both find the prospect of a broken butt hilarious.)

NEIL. We definitely do not need a broken butt. I like yr butt the way it is. I love you the way you are.

(The men kiss.)

JESSE. "Iowa, Kansas, Kentucky, Louisiana, Maine…"

*(**NEIL** joins.)*

JESSE/NEIL. "Maryland, Massachusetts, Michigan—"

*(The sound of breaking glass and then—**NEIL** is gone.)*

JESSE. I believe that there are things you should always do. You should always splash in puddles. You should always ask the kids turning ropes on the corner if you can 'jump in.' You should walk barefoot through grass and dance on beaches. You should do these things for no real reason except that sometimes it is necessary. Sometimes our bodies, our spirits, need a release. Sometimes, and I learned this from Neil, all you can do is throw back yr head… Throw back yr head and—

(He yells. Loud. Long. Deep.)

In moments of great pain I think about something that the poet Essex Hemphill once said: "Take Care Of Yr Blessings." And I count them.

One: I was given a mind and the ability to think.
Two: I have the ability to put my thoughts on paper.
Three: I have known love.

> *(He takes a moment, as long as he needs, and then—.)*

Sometimes I wish I were just like everyone else. Subject to the same gravitational pull. Sometimes I wish I knew how to ride a bike.

> *(Beat.)*

Sometimes I wish that it all made just a little more sense. The bottle. The blood. Neil not being here with me.

> *(Beat.)*

Sometimes...

> *(Beat.)*

But this is where we are. Here and now. And wishes... like jabberwocks and gryphons, Santa Claus and the Tooth Fairy, are unsubstantial stuff. And so...throw yr heads back, y'all. Promise me you will, okay?
Even after I'm gone? Throw them back. And yell. Yell. Yell. YELL!
Because life is so precious.

> *(Beat.)*

"Take Care Of Yr Blessings."

> *(The lights fade to black.)*

End of Play

www.ingramcontent.com/pod-product-compliance
Ingram Content Group UK Ltd.
Pitfield, Milton Keynes, MK11 3LW, UK
UKHW020710260325
456749UK00008B/954